The Gate of Dreams

To Kendra and Cory
with my warmest wishes,
Lillian S. Moats
1996

May your fondest dreams
come true!

S0-CYD-815

The Gate of Dreams

Stories and Illustrations by

Lillian Somersaulter Moats

Cranbrook Press • Bloomfield Hills, Michigan • 1996

Text © 1992 by Lillian Somersaulter Moats
Illustrations © 1993 by Lillian Somersaulter Moats
All rights reserved

First Edition published 1993
Revised Second Edition published 1996 by

Cranbrook Press
1221 Woodward Avenue • P.O. Box 801
Bloomfield Hills, Michigan • 48303-0801

Library of Congress Catalog Card Number
95-70729

ISBN 0-9636492-1-3

Printed in U.S.A. by Thomson-Shore, Inc.

Dedicated to the beauty of
Cranbrook,

And within it, the joy of
Brookside…

Which, like a gate of dreams,
opened wondrous worlds to me.

AN INTRODUCTION TO THE FAIRY STORIES
by Helen Southgate Williams

Hans Christian Andersen's countryman, Kai Munk, has remarked that there are two kinds of writing: writing of entertainment, which is ephemeral, and writing of existence, which has a life of its own and can be very entertaining as well. I believe that the exquisite fairy tales of Lillian Somersaulter Moats are writings of existence; for all their fantasy they are life — universal, eternal. And with charming lightness, they speak seriously.

These great stories bring to us all the emotions we can respond to—delight, recognition, suspense, gaiety, and surely the emotion that is primal—wonder!

This gifted author-artist has distinguished herself in her choice of settings for her fairy tales, and involves the reader principally by means of allegory. She constructs her settings from the homey everyday details, evoking a sense of intimacy which she maintains throughout her tales.

I first met the author when she was ten years old. Her mother, who had heard of my dedication to children and books, brought Lillian to me along with some of her poems and stories. I was amazed at her insights and her sense of joy. If one can really pinpoint the moment when one discovers rare talent, I found that perhaps I was experiencing that magical moment.

I have watched with pleasure and astonishment her development into a gifted writer. Her stories beg to be shared with children, for they are little masterpieces.

Helen Southgate Williams
Honorary Member of The International Board on Books for Young People (IBBY), lecturer, teacher and literary consultant

AN INTRODUCTION TO THE ARTWORK
by Glen Michaels

As I look back at the artistic development of Lillian Somersaulter Moats, I am struck by the logic of its progression. As a student at the Young People's Art Center of the Cranbrook Academy of Art, Lillian explored every medium to the fullest. Her keen eye was able to focus on minute detail, without ever losing the total vision. Her relentless pursuit of perfection never stopped. These qualities have served her well for two decades as an award-winning filmmaker. Now her filmic skills and disciplines are, in turn, enriching her talents as an illustrator.

As in film, the silhouette characters in THE GATE OF DREAMS perform the stories, making text and illustrations wholly supportive of each other. Lillian not only accepts the challenge silhouettes present to the illustrator, she makes them work for her as an ideal way to follow her stories.

The international acclaim won by her films has been richly deserved. This, her first book, promises to be the beginning of a new and different way for Lillian to enrich and engage the minds and senses of the young and old alike.

Glen Michaels

Architectural sculptor, painter, Director of The Cranbrook Academy of Art's Young People's Art Center (1958-1965), recipient of the Michigan Foundation for the Arts Award

A "Note to Parents, Grandparents and Teachers"
by Lillian Somersaulter Moats
directly follows the stories.

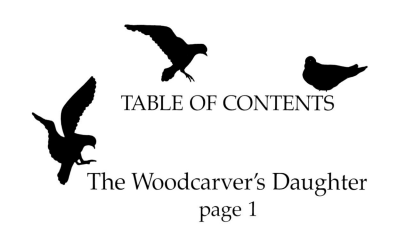

TABLE OF CONTENTS

The Woodcarver's Daughter

THE WOODCARVER'S DAUGHTER

The woodcarver loved the woodland where he lived. He hated city strife. He loved his baby daughter, and he loved his wife. In many ways, he was a simple man. But none who had ever seen the intricacy of his woodcarving could dispute his brilliance.

The creatures of the woodland did not flee the sound of the woodcarver's approach. For they had spied him as a youth crouching upon the forest floor to carve his inspirations. And he had stirred in them a mysterious longing to be caught for all time in the work of his hands. Soon the lore of him had spread to the birds in the skies above the woodland, and to the fish in the deep clear waters of the woodland lakes. Indeed, because of the depth of their longing, time blinked for the woodland creatures, so that mid-stream, mid-flight, mid-stride, mid-fight they could hold fast in stark and stunning poses for the woodcarver.

THE GATE OF DREAMS

Strange as it may seem to us here and now, it was common knowledge there and then, that the loveliest trees of the woodland beckoned to the woodcarver as he sought wood for each new carving. Alder and cherry, linden and elm would gladly sacrifice their limbs and even their lives, to be transformed by his shaping hand for ever and ever.

As word of the woodcarver's talent spread from the woodland to the city, he was called upon to adorn the most important cathedrals and grandest edifices of the land. Like his eager spirit, his shadow preceded him as he strode west to his labor in the town each morning. But as he returned, yearning for his family each evening, his shadow lengthened and reached out for the woodland with his stride.

At dusk, his wife held their baby daughter while she listened at the forest's edge for the "swish, swish" of her husband's footsteps in the meadow grass. In a fond and favorite game, the woodcarver's wife would set down their tiny daughter just as her husband's shadow touched them. And the child would toddle the shadow's length to be swept up in her father's embrace.

But one day the woodcarver did not find his wife and child at the forest's edge. Suddenly his heart was gripped with darkness as his stride lengthened into a run. "Hasten home," the trees whispered. "Faster," they urged him. On the porch of his cottage, the woodcarver saw a neighbor woman holding his child. He flew through the door to find his wife lying feverish in their bed. Though he cared for her devotedly, before many days had passed, the woodcarver's wife closed her eyes forever.

In the lonely evenings that followed, the man amused his baby with lovely toys which he carved for her. Such a responsive child was she that her laughter softened his grief, and he began to take his daughter with him, even to his labor. After a time, the woodcarver was summoned to work at the castle whose broad wings spread like a soaring bird across the hillside overlooking the town. Only the finest artisans in all of Europe were called by the Queen to work there. So that when he received an invitation, the woodcarver accepted at once.

"I will gladly serve you," he said, kneeling before the Queen, "but I must bring my daughter with me as there is no one else to care for her." The Queen was only too delighted, for she had taken a fancy to the little toddler at first sight. And so it was that the woodcarver closed the beloved cottage he and his wife had shared, and moved into lodgings in the heart of the town.

  Everyone at the castle was enchanted with the spirited ways of the woodcarver's daughter. At her father's feet, she loved to play in the wood shavings, gathering them up in her pinafore and spilling them over her head, until her dark hair was festooned with golden curls. When the roving minstrels played their fiddles, their notes drew the woodcarver's daughter to her toes. For though her little legs were newly upright, she could not keep them still when she heard a note of music. The Queen herself took notice of this, as she observed everything about the little girl; and thenceforth instruction by the finest dancers in the kingdom was provided for the child.

As the years passed, the girl came to be admired for her energy and grace by everyone at court. In looks alone she was no more lovely than this one or that one. But when the woodcarver's daughter danced, all eyes fell upon her. She was light as a tuft of cottonwood on a breeze, nimble as a leaf in the rapids, supple as a tendril on a vine, quiet as snow.

Now there was a woman in the city who took a particular interest in the stories the woodcarver told of the life he and his daughter found at the castle. She was an ambitious woman, believing that wealth and celebrity had thus far been denied to her only because she lacked connections at the royal court. Her true colors were as inscrutable as a chameleon's. But at her heart of hearts she hid the green of envy, the crimson of rage.

The woman tried at first to make the woodcarver lose his heart to her. But the woodcarver had no interest in marrying again and in his eyes the woman's advances went unnoticed. If the woodcarver had spurned the woman, she might have turned away from him in her wrath. But since he merely ignored her, she became more determined to use his daughter as her entrée to the Queen. She began to play upon the man's guilt by saying, "Your daughter will be growing into young womanhood one day. It is unnatural for her to spend all of her time with you. She will be needing a woman's care." The woman led the woodcarver to believe that she had taken a fond interest in his child. So that when she offered to stay in his house and serve as governess to his daughter, the poor woodcarver consented, believing he was doing the very best for his offspring.

At first the new governess treated the girl rather well, for the conniving woman was sure that she had obtained the key to the Queen's own heart. When the woman begged the woodcarver to carve a doll in the likeness of his daughter, the man took the woman's request to be genuinely fond. But secretly, the governess planned to advance herself at court by presenting the doll as a personal gift to the Queen.

The woodcarver took such care over the little replica of his daughter that it grew more perfect each day. When it was finally complete, it had become so exquisite that it quite surpassed the child's own beauty.

The governess had not found fault with the spritely child before she saw the perfect doll. But from that day on she gave the girl no peace, for the woman was constantly trying to improve her. The governess scrutinized the child's appearance, criticized her speech, and picked at her dancing until the girl lost the natural blush of her cheek, the flow of her thoughts, and the lift of her step.

Then, failing to make the child exactly like the doll, and angered by the girl's dwindling spirit, the governess began to fear that the Queen, herself, might soon lose interest in the child. "The girl must stay at home today," she announced to the father, "for she has become ill." Taking his child's trembling and reticence as confirmation of her ill health, the woodcarver kissed her tenderly and set out without her for the castle. Later that morning, unbeknownst to the woodcarver, the governess, too, made her way to the castle with the exquisite doll ornately wrapped as a gift to the Queen.

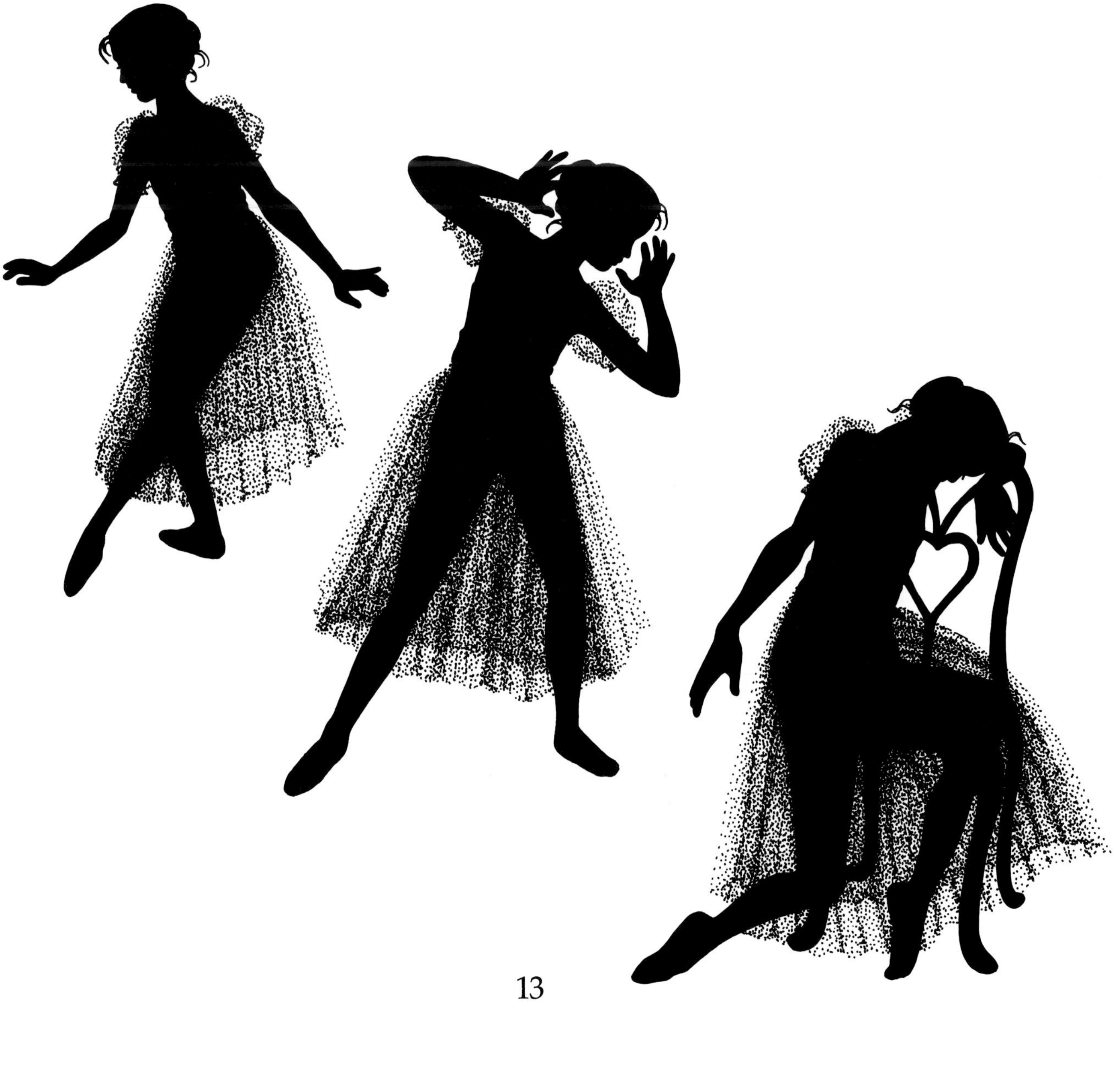

"It is extraordinary!" the Queen exclaimed. "Utterly perfect!" But the wise Queen was not easily fooled by those who were bent on winning her favor, so she added, "It is really *too* perfect to be a portrait of the little girl I have come to love. And besides, the figure cannot move...how can it capture the spirit of a child who is movement itself?"

The governess was bitterly disappointed for she had been certain she could impress the Queen with such a priceless gift. And as she returned home, her heart blackened with spite.

She pounded the little replica on the child's own bureau and laughed a cruel laugh. "There! See what you are not!" she said. She commanded the child to dance, but she could not, for her movements had become stiff and wooden. The governess badgered and belittled the girl until, in fact, she did become ill... so ill, that she lay quite motionless in her bed day after day.

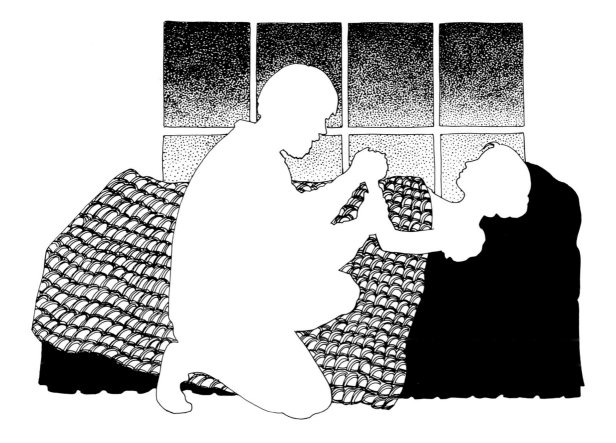

Soon the girl no longer spoke at all. The woodcarver knew nothing of what the cruel governess was doing to his child; and the finest doctors could find neither cause nor cure for her ill-health. So the woodcarver sat by his beloved daughter's bedside night after night and tried to cheer her by carving fanciful little toys for her amusement. But she rarely looked at them. She seemed always to be looking elsewhere, to be looking inward. Each morning, before the woodcarver left for the castle, he went to the girl's bedside and kissed her forehead as she slept. Months passed, and the child's health only worsened.

Then, in the half-light of a winter morning, as the woodcarver approached his daughter's bed and bent to kiss her brow, he was horror struck....

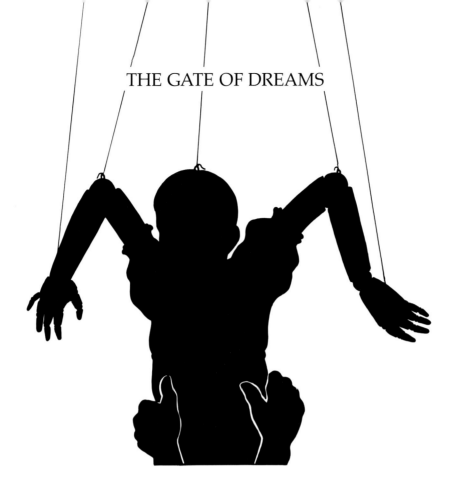

THE GATE OF DREAMS

For in the night his beloved child had changed altogether, into a wooden marionette! And there it lay in the child's own image and proportion, dressed in her sleeping gown. The father wept and moaned so loudly as he knelt at her bedside, that the wicked governess awakened and ran into the bedroom to see.

When she beheld the marionette, so like the girl in every way, she shouted for joy. Without stopping to think, she blurted out, "At last I have the perfect gift to win the Queen's heart. For this puppet's likeness is exact, and I have only to work the strings to make it dance for her. I'll take it to the Queen this very day!"

When the poor woodcarver heard the woman's callous words, he clutched the marionette to his heart and banished the governess from his house forever. She lunged for the marionette's wand, but the father held fast to the puppet so that —snap! The strings broke from the wand in her hand. Raging, the woman skulked from the house. In its shadows she waited until she saw the woodcarver depart with the marionette cradled in his arms.

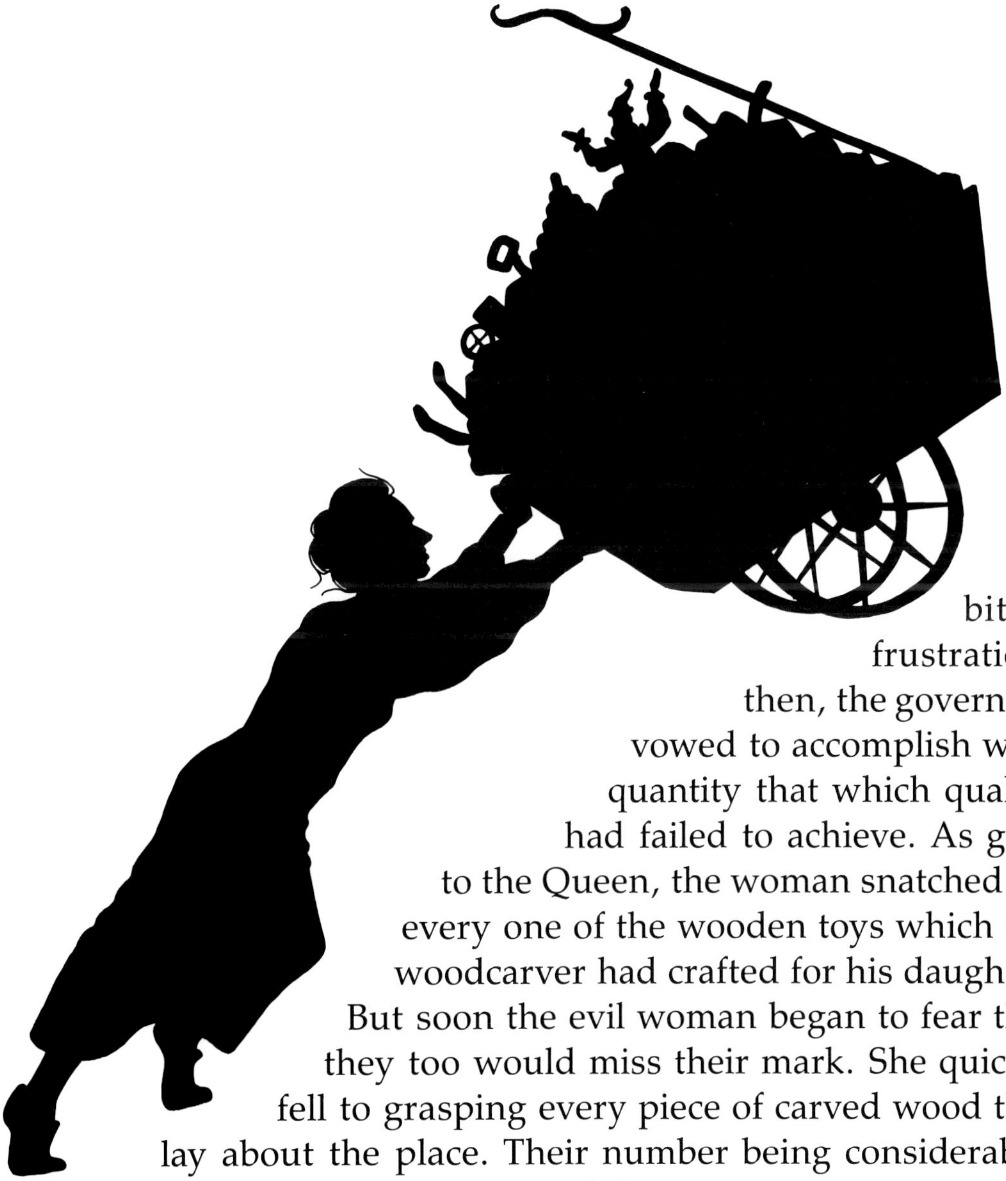

In bitter frustration, then, the governess vowed to accomplish with quantity that which quality had failed to achieve. As gifts to the Queen, the woman snatched up every one of the wooden toys which the woodcarver had crafted for his daughter. But soon the evil woman began to fear that they too would miss their mark. She quickly fell to grasping every piece of carved wood that lay about the place. Their number being considerable, she heaped them like a bountiful mountain upon a wooden cart. With great exertion she pushed it, straining against the steep grade of the road leading to the castle. But just outside the castle gates one of the carvings toppled to the ground. As the greedy governess bent to retrieve it, the overladen cart rolled back upon her, crushing her like kindling beneath its wheels.

All of this time, the woodcarver had wandered with the marionette in his arms until his weary footsteps carried him to the familiar woodland. The wooden limbs of the puppet clattered with the rhythm of the father's steps and the snow crunched under his feet. At the sound of his approach, the creatures of the forest bowed their heads to the woodcarver and held their reverent poses until he had passed. Then at a respectful distance, they followed like devoted servants. As the woodcarver passed the empty cottage where he had once lived in happiness with his wife and baby daughter, he wept anew. Wandering deeper and deeper into the forest, at last he came upon a frozen lake. Near the jagged rocks that bordered it, he collapsed in exhaustion upon the ice.

It happened then that a young woodsman who had come to fish there, skated onto the ice. And when he saw the poor woodcarver bent by the rocks in despair, he glided swiftly to him. As the older man lifted his head, the woodsman beheld the wooden face of the marionette, now wet with the father's tears.

The young man said, "When I was a little boy there lived in this forest a woodcarver of great talent. If the beautiful puppet is of your own making, you must, indeed, be he!"

Overcome, the father buried his face in his hand and told his sorrowful tale to the woodsman. The young woodsman was so moved by the woodcarver's story that he longed to relieve the poor man of his plight. But in his helplessness, the young man could only take a sharp rock and strike it hard upon the ice until it broke the surface. Sadly he said, "I wish I could do more than to catch a fish for your supper."

Before the young woodsman could drop his line into the water, however, there sprang above the surface a golden fish so beautiful and rare that neither man had ever before seen its likeness. From the water's very depths it had been drawn by the presence of the woodcarver. And now it held still for him in a lithe and artful pose, its long fins swept round about it, cloaking its mysteries. Taking the wondrous fish gently in his hands, the father said, "I would carve your image in the castle gates if only you would share with me your wisdom from the deep. Help me, wise fish, for I cannot understand what has happened to my beloved daughter."

Then the fish found a voice like crystal chimes and spoke to him,

"Woodcarver, woodcarver, brokenhearted,
Wondering how this trouble started,
Recollect a little doll,
For tragedy can start out small."

The woodcarver's face paled at the fish's words, and the young woodsman looked at him imploringly for an explanation. But the father only stared, transfixed, into the water's depths as he murmured, "...the little doll I carved...the likeness of my daughter...."
Then the wise fish spoke again,

"Soon this window to the deep
Will close and all its secrets keep.
If you can fathom what to do
Before the window seals anew,
Then you shall give your child the chance
To live and breathe—once more to dance!"

Breaking from its perfect pose, the fish suddenly slipped into the watery hole. The poor father longed to beseech the fish to return. But he could only gaze immobilized into the depths.

Over the young woodsman's face apprehension swept, as he watched the edges of the hole, this precious window to the deep, turn from transparency to translucency. Gripping the woodcarver's shoulder, he tried to break the man's trance, but it was no use. "Quickly!" he whispered to himself. "I must hurry to the woodcarver's lodgings and bring back to him the little doll." But as the young man tore off his skates, he feared he would never make it back before the ice froze over, for the way to the city was arduous by foot.

As if it had read the young man's worried heart, a noble stag quietly stepped forth from the lake's edge and knelt before him. Instantly the woodsman leapt upon the creature's back; and leaning onto the stag's mighty neck, he grasped its crown of antlers. "Show me the way," he cried as the stag lunged into the deep twilight. The woodland trees bent their boughs to clear a path. "Hasten," they whispered. "Faster," they urged. The young man's heart quickened as the stag's rapid hooves crackled through the underbrush, pounded over the meadow, thundered over the cobblestone streets of the castle town and finally clattered to a halt before a modest dwelling.

Springing from the stag's back, the woodsman was certain that he had been transported to the woodcarver's lodgings. But when he found the door ajar and threw it open, his heart sank; for the place had been stripped of any evidence that a woodcarver had ever resided there. From room to room the young man raced, finding not a single wooden carving. Then just as he resolved to go on searching through the town for the woodcarver's true dwelling, he saw a little room at the back of the house and looked in. And there, on the girl's bureau where the cruel governess had scorned it, stood the extraordinary little doll.

Clasping the carving to his breast as a priceless treasure, the young woodsman sprang onto the stag's mighty back once more and held fast to the antlers with one hand. "Back to the woodcarver," he cried. Night had fallen and brought with it a deeper chill as the moon cast haunting shadows over the city. But only the picture he beheld in his mind's eye had the power to haunt the young woodsman. For in it he could see the constricting edges of the watery hole turning from translucency to opacity. "Faster!" he cried. The stag's fleet hooves darted like lightning over the cobblestone streets of the town, pelted over the meadow, thrashed through the woodland underbrush, and sparked to a halt near the rocks by the lake's very edge.

There the young man found the woodcarver still bent over the ice. The black hole from which the fish had leapt had shrunk and all but closed, and yet the woodcarver was still transfixed by it. It had become to him a dark looking glass into the past, wherein he could see all that had happened to his daughter. The young woodsman thrust the little doll directly into the father's hands to break his reverie. And tenderly did the young man take the marionette into his own.

For an instant the father stared in horror at the little doll, which once he had taken every care to perfect. Then, just as the frosted edges of the hole converged at last, a look of deepest passion came over the woodcarver's face.

Raising the little carving high above his head, he cried in his anguish, *"My daughter alive meant more to me than all my perfect dreams!"* Furiously the woodcarver hurled the exquisite doll onto the jagged rocks beside him, splitting the perfect carving in two.

At that very instant, the young man looked down at the marionette in his arms. To his wonderment, the puppet's tangled strings began to melt away. The fine grain of the wood faded as the polished surface softened and warmed to his touch. Then suddenly the marionette stirred in the young man's arms. Never before had the woodsman seen such grace as when, setting the girl down upon her feet, she leapt—and in her dance for joy, her feet barely skimmed the surface of the lake.

So eager to be near her was he that instantly he fastened on his skates and glided to her, lifting her high above him. Then, as he gently set her down, their eyes met for a glistening instant before the young girl darted back to her father. The daughter threw her arms around the woodcarver's neck and kissed his brow. The father's heart leapt too. And so grateful was he to the woodsman, that he invited the young man to visit him often in the city.

When the father and daughter returned to the castle, they heard the tale of the cruel governess's demise from the Queen herself, who now had a perfect story to tell anyone who tried to gain her favor by trickery.

From that day forth, the woodcarver's daughter danced with extraordinary mastery. Her gracefulness was sung near and abroad, so that many a noble prince journeyed to the castle to ask for her hand in marriage. But when at last she was moved to wed, the hand she chose was the very one that had helped to free her. And so the young woodsman and the woodcarver's daughter lived together in happiness for the rest of their days.

Franz the Fool

FRANZ THE FOOL

*L*ong ago, when magic often woke while mortals slept, a boy named Franz lived with his father on a lofty mountain's slope. Lovingly the boy looked up at the snowcapped peaks all around him—peaks that yearned for and sometimes reached the clouds. The days he cherished most were those when snowy crests and clouds combined in ever changing artistry. "Stop daydreaming!" the father would snap at his little son. "There's work to be done!"

It seemed to Franz that his neighbors rarely looked beyond the dark spruce forests that circled their mountain town. Growing up amongst such plentiful wood, his father had become a carpenter, and had decided that Franz should be a carpenter too. Every tool his father gave to him the boy quickly mastered, yet in his heart he could find no love of wood.

Years passed as the youth worked under his father's guidance, but on winter nights by lantern light Franz began to labor alone, carving his vivid dreams out of towering blocks of ice. Alas, he toiled through the long winter, only to watch his work melt in the springtime sun. The villagers watched too. And when one of them whispered, *"Franz, the fool!"*, how the joke did travel!

Not wanting to be the father of a fool, the carpenter distanced himself from his only child. Year after year, the tattling tongues of the villagers flickered like serpents. Yet none of their insults was as hurtful to Franz as the words of his own father. "You will never grow up to be one of us," he scoffed. "You are only a foolish dreamer!"

One cloudswept winter night when Franz had grown into young manhood, he dreamt of a gentle young woman waiting before a gate of doves. There was such a simple elegance about her that the young man awakened from his dream, and set to work that very night carving her image. Franz had never felt so unequal to a task, for how could he convey in ice the warmth of her expression?

When the statue was complete, it was indeed no rival for the wondrous image imprinted on the young man's mind. Yet the lovely statue outshone any he had ever before created. Even the sculpted folds of drapery appeared to riffle in the wind. For the young man's hands were adept. And in his mind's eye, he had frozen in time the inspiring pose that had stirred his sleep.

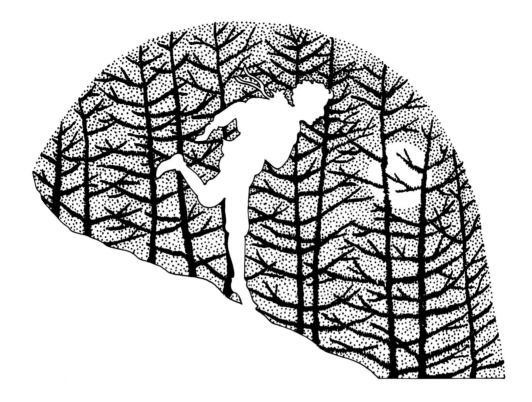

In the harsh light of morning the villagers found the statue and laughed more loudly than ever. "That is the only girl who would ever have Franz the Fool," they chided. "Now he has outdone himself!" All through the winter their whispers tormented him like the hissing of vipers, until he vowed that when spring came he would leave the village forever.

The days grew longer and the sun grew hotter. Finally, Franz's statue began to melt. "Look what Franz's sweetheart is doing—she's running away from him!" the villagers jeered.

Franz longed to have something by which to remember his beautiful statue. It happened that a tiny vessel of silver had been left to him by his mother before she died. So in this precious bottle, engraved with the simple emblem of a snowdrop flower, he collected some of the water that now glistened in a pool at the statue's feet. Late that night, as the whole village slept, he packed the silver bottle along with a few belongings. And at the bedroom door of his slumbering father, he bid a silent sad farewell.

Afraid of losing his courage, Franz bolted down the mountain pathway until his legs throbbed with the rhythm of his aching heart. Only then did the young man realize that he had never thought beyond his own escape. Sitting down upon a rock, he took the silver vessel from his belongings, intending to use the precious water only to moisten his parched lips. But no sooner had he opened the bottle than his thirst was mysteriously quenched. Suddenly, startlingly, the soft voice of a young woman spoke to him, *"As soon as you rise to your feet, Franz, you will know which way to travel."* The young man looked all about him but there was not another soul in sight. Could the beautiful voice have come from within the vessel... from the very waters of his lost statue?

Trembling, Franz tucked the tiny bottle into his belongings as he rose to his feet. Then, indeed, he did feel strangely certain that he knew which way to go. On and on he journeyed, as the air grew warmer each day. Surely his chosen path was leading him to a land where there might be no ice even in winter. And yet Franz held firm to his conviction.

As dawn swept across the meadow grass one morning, Franz awakened to find that dark clouds had gathered over a nearby forest. There was a scent of smoke in the air. Though he could not have answered why, the young man hastened into the woods to find the source of the billowing smoke. Above the forest, a swarm of birds screeched through the skies. But since their own survival drove both predator and prey, the goshawk spared the darting shrew below him. The owl passed the dormouse by. Running contrary to every creature fleeing the forest, Franz came upon a clearing where he found a village ablaze.

How it tore at his heart to see the work of the villagers' hands being destroyed. Tirelessly he battled the blaze beside the strangers, though white heat and rolling blackness pressed them back and back toward the woods. When at last the villagers broke away in exhaustion, Franz turned aside for a moment and opened the silver bottle he cherished. Once more his thirst was quenched without a drink. And again the quiet voice spoke to him: *"Cast several drops of me to the sky, Franz, and I shall call upon my sisters."*

Franz hurled a few of the beloved drops into the air—and the heavens remarked with a clap of thunder! Instantly, he felt cold raindrops falling all about him. These multiplied until they fell in torrents upon the flames, and thereby the beloved village square was saved.

Into their weary throng the villagers swept the helpful stranger, though they did not know that it was he who had summoned the rain for them. So moved was Franz that he offered to help the villagers rebuild their houses. For this kindness they would have repaid him in any way they could. But he wanted nothing except their permission to build a little cottage next to the murmuring river that wound through the forest near their town.

The next morning, with thinning clouds of smoke and steam still swirling at their feet, Franz and the villagers searched through the rubble. In the pitiful remains of many houses, something caught the young man's eye. Simple doorways still stood arched over the ashes that had once been doors. "What are these entranceways made of?" Franz inquired.

"Marble," answered the villagers. And they told Franz that, nestled in the hills nearby, was a quarry of snow white stone. Seeing how the substance charmed the young man's mind, the grateful villagers brought large pieces of it to him, never knowing to what purpose he would apply their gifts.

Only under the protective cloak of night did Franz begin to sculpt his visions in marble. For he was certain that he would have the villagers' friendship only as long as he hid from them the dreams which had always brought him scorn. The difficulty of learning to sculpt in marble, and the melancholy of his memories, were sometimes too much for Franz. On such desolate nights even the clinking of his own chisel seemed to taunt him. For as its ringing echoed against the trees, the music proclaimed a score of craftsmen laboring in harmony. But when Franz stopped his work to listen, the stunning silence confirmed to him that he was utterly alone.

Then he would take the top from the little vessel, and the silvery voice would sing out to him, *"Do not despair, Franz. I am with you still."*

By day, as he worked with the villagers, the dappled shadows of sunlit leaves veiled the marble forms in his secret forest. But at night, in Franz's lonely presence, the moonlight heightened the lovely contrast between snow white and forest green. The silent moon lent its silvery glow to every figure the young man crafted among the trees.

It was not long before the woods behind Franz's dwelling were peopled with marble figures, captured in the fleeting poses Franz collected from his dreams. In a silver birch tree, he placed upon a branch the sculpted form of a winged boy, who cast a wistful smile at the figures of his wingless brothers, wrestling in the fronds beneath.

Arising from the hollow base of a fallen oak, Franz fashioned the frightening figure of an ancient falconer. The statue's gloved hand pointed toward the marble falcon which swooped down upon the figure of a fleeing youth. In the instant Franz portrayed, the falcon's talons pierced the young boy's flesh, transforming the statue's marble arm into a marble branch. The figure's fingers turned to sculpted twigs with sprouting leaves. And on the face of the tormented youth, Franz carved an agonizing backward glance.

THE GATE OF DREAMS

In the shallow river bed, the statue of a young girl sat upon a rock. Her head was bent above an open book. Her marble fingers trailed through the rippling waters. Upon the river's bank, Franz placed a sculpted form, half man, half mountain goat, so near the girl that she might have felt its gaze upon her back. But the marble creature hid its human face behind two cloven hands.

Franz's imagination was more charmed by the translucent marble than ever it had been by ice. At the edge of his secret forest, he carved in tribute to the dream spirit whose soft voice now sustained him, the most beautiful gate of sculpted marble doves. They descended from its arch in rhythmic waves, and alighted at its base in quietude.

Though the young man allowed himself to take the top from the silver vessel only when he most yearned for inspiration, some of the precious water escaped as vapor with every opening. And at last there came a night when the vessel seemed to him as light as air. Franz's heart sank in his chest. Opening the vessel with quaking hands, the young man strained to hear the words that the familiar voice now whispered, *"Pour these last drops onto the ground, and your gain shall be far dearer than your loss."*

"Impossible!" Franz cried. "How could I let you disappear into the dry earth?"

Dwindling with every word, the gentle voice answered him, *"The time has come, Franz, when to keep me you must cast me away."*

With an aching heart, Franz called forth his faltering courage, and did, at last, as the voice had bid him. Then in amazement, he fell to his knees. For the last precious droplets were not absorbed as he had imagined. Instead, they arranged themselves into a tiny circle and lay glistening atop the ground. Hoping for another sign, perhaps another word, Franz could not take his eyes away. The night passed as he kept his vigil, but the droplets neither moved nor spoke again. At last in weary desperation Franz fell asleep upon the chill ground.

When dawn broke, he did not awaken as he had each morning to work with the villagers. Hours passed, and as the sun rose high in the sky it warmed the forest floor. But Franz did not hear the rustling in the leaves nearby as a viper stirred itself.

When afternoon came and at last dusk fell, the villagers' puzzlement at Franz's absence deepened to concern. "He has merely taken a day of needed rest," one elder voice assured the others. "We will doubtless see Franz again at dawn." Since none of the grateful villagers wanted to intrude upon his privacy, a young woman's soft voice went unheeded, saying, "But Franz would never disappoint us without a word." Failing to make her gentle insight heard, the girl slipped away from her elders and set out, lantern in hand, to find the young man. When she reached his cottage, night had fallen, cooling the forest once more.

In waves the viper slipped from the rock upon which it had sunned itself, and slithered unknowingly toward Franz; for in the darkness its scale-clad eyes could only detect motion.

Once, twice, three times the young girl knocked on Franz's door. But there was no response. Shyly, she entered the house. But therein her light revealed no sign of Franz.

Further on, at the edge of the forest, illuminated by moonlight, she beheld a gate—the beautiful marble arch of flocking doves. The girl felt as if she were in a dream, for she had never seen anything like it before. At the gate she called, "Franz!" and waited for an answer. Still Franz did not awaken.

The serpent wound a path amongst the leaves, its flickering tongue seeking a way through the darkness. Suddenly the snake sensed the warmth of Franz's body and swayed its threatening head from side to side. The young girl's gaze alighted on the viper just as it hissed and drew back its head to strike.

"Franz, Franz!" the girl cried in horror as she darted through the arched gate.

But no sooner had she passed under it, than she was startled by a thunderous beating of wings. The flocking doves, which had been sculpted in marble, took flight into the starry sky, pulsing the night. The viper vanished for an instant in the leaves, until a pair of doves, parting from their sisters in the sky, swooped down to the forest floor. Catching a supple branch between their beaks, they swept it over the snake's half hidden form. The angry viper rose and struck at last, sinking its poison fangs deep within the branch's woody flesh. Then up, up into the moonlit sky soared the doves with the serpent lashing between them, like a harmless ribbon in the wind.

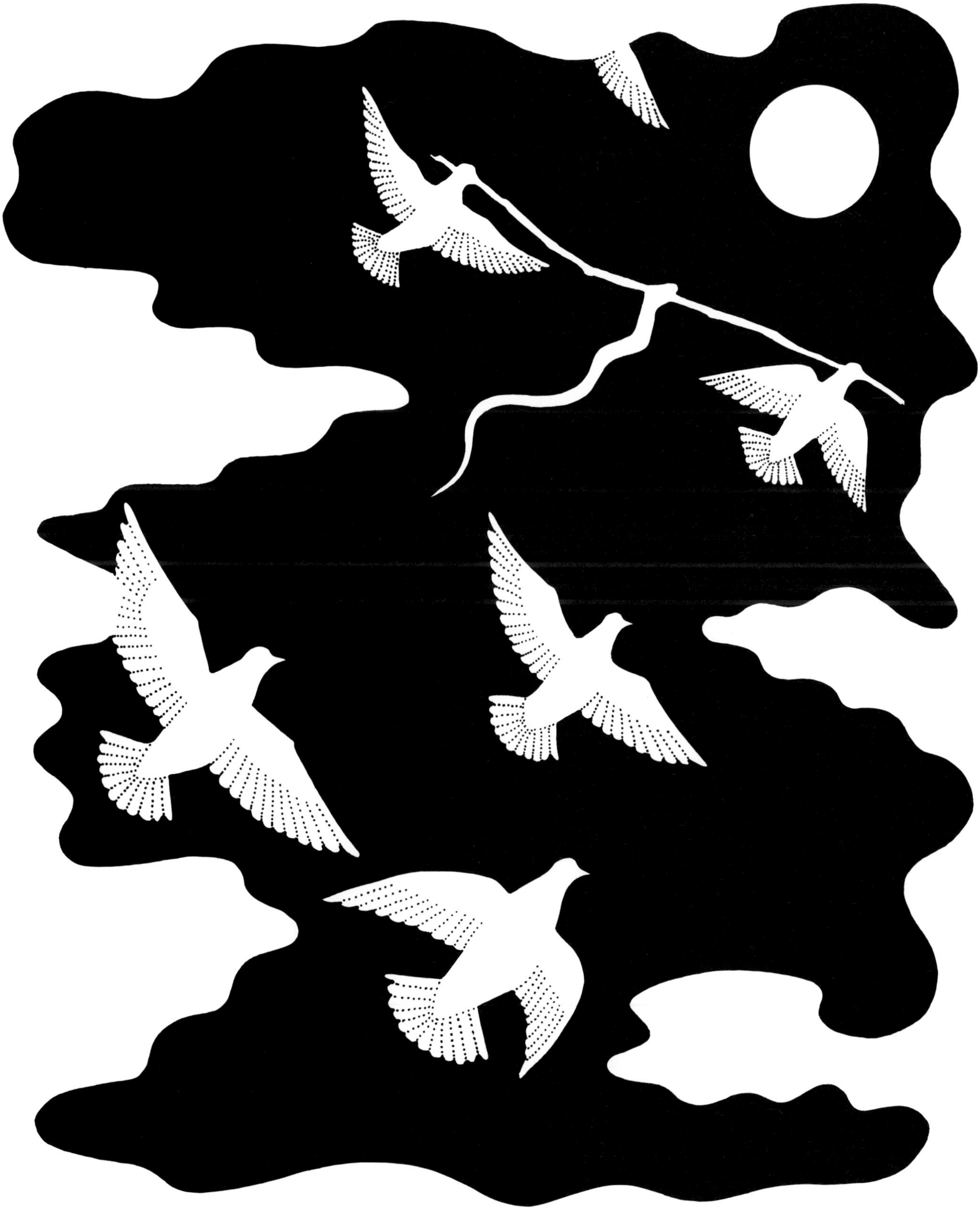

The clamor of wings awakened Franz. But when at last he was fully drawn from the deepest well of sleep, his eyes beheld only the young woman standing where the gate had been. His waking heart wanted to soar like the doves. But it could only pound in his chest, for it seemed to Franz that his whole life was being laid bare to the girl. Slowly she glided towards him, her eyes widening as she beheld each moonlit figure amongst the trees. Franz lay frozen in his posture of sleep until, at last, the young girl knelt beside him. "Oh, Franz," she cried, her frightened eyes searching his, "how near you came to dying in the midst of all this loveliness." And her cheeks were wet with tears.

Franz felt himself melt at the sound of her voice as softly she told him all that she had seen through the gate of doves. Lifting his hand from the place where it had rested as he slept, he touched the young girl's cheek. Instantly, a glint of light flashed from the ground. And in the very spot where the last precious droplets of water had gathered, a circle of tiny diamonds glistened in their place.

As Franz reached out in awe to touch the jewels, they joined together in a silver setting. He took the mysterious ring in his hand. It was as cold as ice and as brilliant as starlight. Gently he pressed it between the girl's palm and his own until it drew warmth from them. And Franz and the young woman looked at one another in wonderment!

In the joyous days that followed, the circlet of diamonds became their wedding ring. Franz eagerly shared with his bride his only family heirloom, the precious vessel of silver. Though it was empty, he found himself forever filled with the inspiration it had once contained. Though it was silent, it would always convey the story of how their love began. In the heart of the village, Franz and the young woman were married with the townspeople encircling them in candlelight. In the joyous procession that followed, the bride proudly led her people to the secret sculpture, for she had persuaded her lover that he must no longer hide his work away.

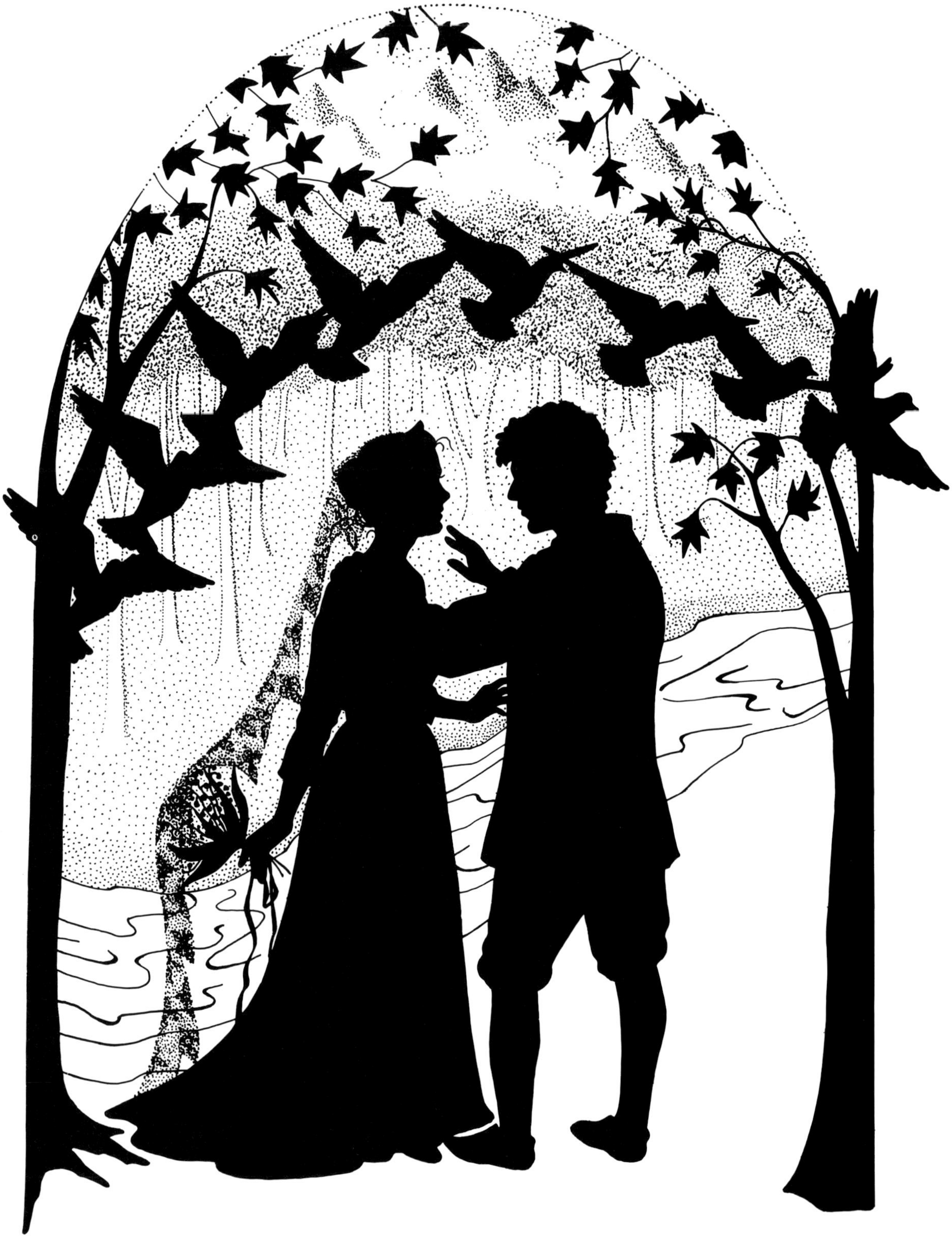

When the villagers beheld their gifts of marble so artfully transformed, their love for Franz swelled with admiration. In the years that followed, the fond nickname which the villagers gave to the forest of sculpture was heard far and wide. When spring came each year, melting the ice from the distant snowcapped mountaintop, the bubbling river ran down through the wondrous forest murmuring its name....

"The Gate..." the river whispered. "The Gate of Dreams."

The Girl of the Bells

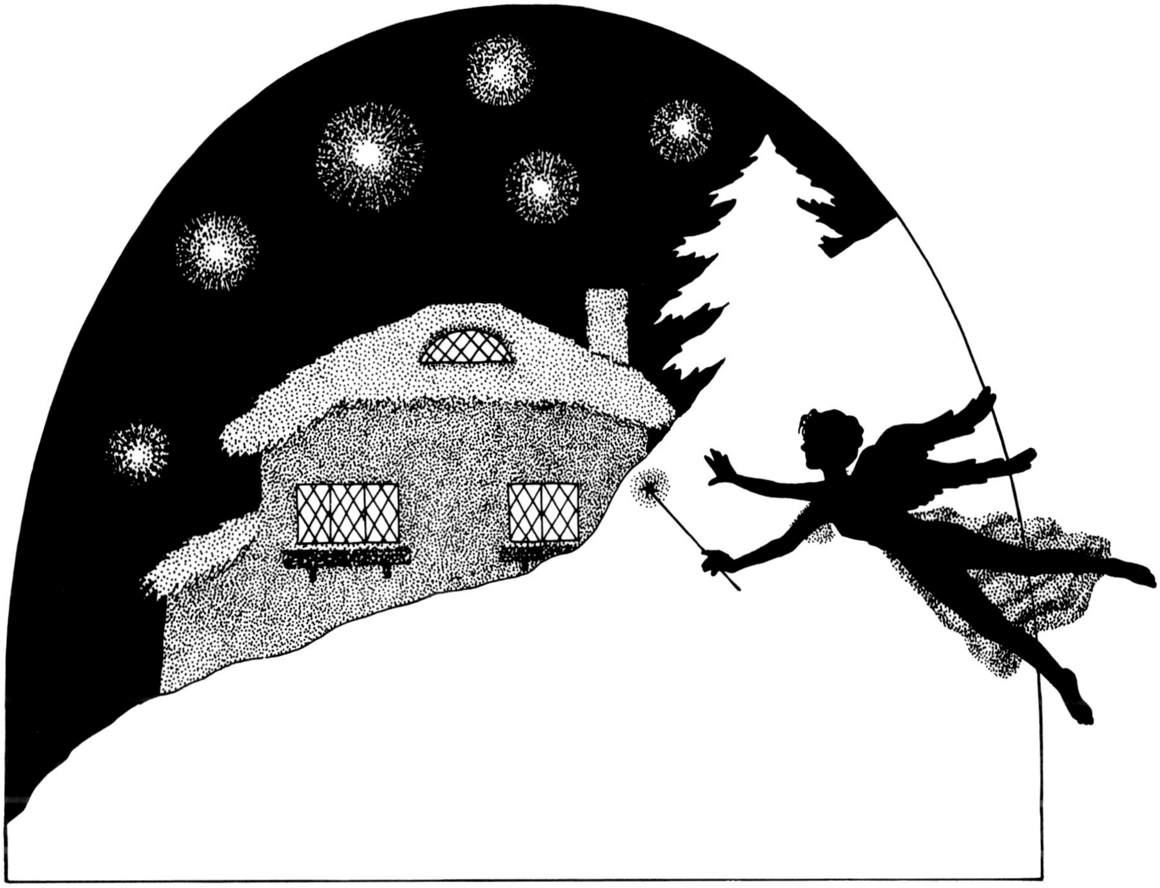

THE GIRL OF THE BELLS

Once, long ago, a night of blackest sky and brightest stars settled over a hillside cottage. There a young shepherd and his beloved wife awaited the birth of their firstborn child. They were two waiting to become three. But three they would never be, for that night the shepherd's wife died giving birth to a lovely daughter. If ever a single night could have torn a heart in two, this was such an eve for the young shepherd.

As he wept and rocked his infant in his arms, a fairy appeared and spoke to him. "Though this poor child shall have no mother, she shall not be poor in love," the fairy said, "for I myself shall see that her life is not unhappy. She shall be called 'Carabella, the girl of the bells'." The fairy then touched the baby's tiny hands and disappeared.

For a time the man was torn between grief and gladness. If his wife had been a flower crushed in full bloom, his daughter became to him a delicate bud unfurling in loveliness day by day. The shepherd called his little daughter "Carabella", and took tender care of her. As time passed, the child grew to love the sound of ringing bells. And she discovered to her delight and wonderment that if she but snapped her fingers she could make a bell appear. Carabella's music soon rang over the hillside. And as the fairy had decreed, she came to be called "the girl of the bells" by all who knew her.

On the hillside each day, Carabella helped her father tend his sheep. In their cottage each evening, she filled the immeasurable silence left by her mother with the rapturous ringing of her bells. But one night the shepherd came to his daughter and said, "You must stay alone tonight, for I need to hunt the wolves that prey upon our flock."

"Will you be safe, Father?" she worried aloud.

"I'll have my gun to protect me," said the shepherd.

"Then what if one of our sheep should wander from the others?" asked Carabella. "Could you not mistake it in the darkness for a wolf and kill a gentle sheep instead?" The girl's brow furrowed with concern. "Wait, Father!" she said, "and I will make a bell for each of them to wear so that you will never mistake them, even in the darkness." And this she did, for it was always with acts of tenderness that the shepherd and his daughter looked after their flock.

The shepherd grew content with his life. His past was full of pleasant memory. His present he passed in the warmth of his daughter's company, and in dreams for her future. But little did the shepherd suspect that someone else was making plans for the girl of the bells.

There lived on the same hillside a young man who was a weaver by trade. Bitterly did he resent his poor lot in life, yet he knew no other craft than this. At his loom he did not weave the dreams of a gentle artisan, but the web of a spider, plotting to catch its prey. He had set his mind upon finding a wife, so that she might carry out the labor he had come to despise. To that end, he had tried to snare one young woman after another, only to be rejected by each in turn. In truth, he had not cared for a single one of them. But when the first woman declined to answer his indifference with love, he approached the next with hidden malice. When the second woman refused to answer malice with love, he approached the third with rancor. And so it went, until with vengeful determination he cast his eye upon Carabella, just as she approached young womanhood.

How fitting it would be if they were to wed, the weaver mused. All of the wool he should ever require would be his, if only the shepherd's daughter would consent to marry him! Perhaps Carabella would have found it in her gracious heart to care for the weaver . . . if ever he had lost himself in the lovely rhythm of shuttle and pedal. If ever he had tried to tell a story in a tapestry . . . then he might have understood Carabella's music. But as it was, he loathed everything she loved. And thus, the shepherd's daughter could find no place in her heart for the bitter young man.

"Neither shall this woman be mine!" he cursed, and his heavy hands beat every thread against the weft until it bristled at his touch. Soon he had set his mind on avenging every past rebuke by tormenting young Carabella. Pounding the crank to tighten his warp, he racked his spiteful mind to craft a suitable revenge.

One day the shepherd made the mistake of telling the weaver he would go hunting for wolves that night. At twilight the evil young man removed the bell from one of the lambs and shooed it into the woods. In the darkness before dawn the shepherd took his gun to the forest. A crackling in the underbrush caught his ear. Glimpsing a coat of gray, he aimed and fired his gun. Then, hearing the creature fall to the ground, the shepherd ran to the thicket to make certain the menacing wolf was dead. How his poor heart sickened when he discovered instead—a lifeless lamb.

Walking home with heavy steps, he spied the weaver near his garden gate. "I can hardly bear to tell Carabella what has happened," said the shepherd to his neighbor. As he listened, the weaver did unthinkingly what he had often done in boyhood. One by one he plucked the delicate blossoms of the vinca vine, sucking the nectar contained in each before tossing it to the ground. While feigning sympathy for the shepherd, the cruel young man began to crave even greater revenge. For the outcome of his trickery seemed no more satisfying to him than the paltry measure of nectar from a single tiny flower.

Wearily, the shepherd made his way home, and gently he awakened his daughter. Straining for words, he told her how he had come to kill the poor lamb that had lost its bell. Carabella threw her arms about her father's neck; but at last, unable to hold back her tears, she tore herself from him and ran to the forest to cry alone.

As she lay sobbing on a bed of pine needles, the shepherd's daughter felt something light as gossamer brush her arm. She looked up to find a fairy stooping next to her—the same fairy whom Carabella's father had described to her, time without number. "Do not cry, Carabella," she said. "The day has come for you to follow me."

"Where will you lead me?" asked Carabella.

"I will tell you as we travel," answered the fairy. "Go now, and tell your father goodbye."

On the hillside, Carabella found her father bending over an ancient sheep to soothe its tender hooves. Softly, the shepherd's daughter approached him. "The lovely fairy has come for me, Father," she said, "and I must leave you." Tears filled the shepherd's eyes and he longed to beg Carabella to stay. But remembering that the fairy had long ago promised to make his daughter happy, he softly said, "Yes, you must go now. But remember I am with you, always." The shepherd and his daughter parted with an embrace, and Carabella followed the fairy into the forest.

As the mists rose, every glistening web seemed to be strung with her father's own teardrops. She began to wonder if, until this day, she had peered through the finest veil at life, and listened through the softest blanket of fog. For on this day more was revealed to Carabella than she had ever seen before. Suddenly all things struck her senses like the ringing of crystal!

"Where do you lead me?" whispered Carabella.

"To a land where there is no language but the language of bells," said the fairy.

"But how will I understand what they are saying?" the girl wondered aloud.

"You already know the language," answered the fairy. "Only trust your heart, and you will feel just what to do."

The girl snapped her fingers eight times and an octave of golden bells appeared on a golden rod. Following in the fairy's footsteps, Carabella played until her music was answered by a distant carillon. "The ringing asks, *'Who is it that travels in these woods?'*" Carabella said, delighted that she could understand the meaning of the melody.

"Answer 'Carabella'," said the fairy.

Without a thought, Carabella played a tune on her bells that said her name, and the faraway ringing replied, *"I will come to meet you, Carabella."*

Within moments a young man emerged from the forest and touched the girl's hand. *"We have heard of your magic!"* the young man rang. *"Won't you come and live among us?"*

"I will gladly," she answered, for her heart had quickened to the language of the bells. On the waves of its carillons she traveled with the young man worlds beyond woods, worlds beyond words; until at last in the Land of the Bells she was welcomed by all of its people.

At first, in her new home so foreign and yet familiar, Carabella loved to play her bells in solitude. Yet more and more she longed to make music in harmony with the young man who had led her there. For when she played for him the heartfelt verities, the playful fantasies which she had never sung or spoken but always known, he understood her as readily as if she had struck each chord upon his heart. She could read his understanding in his eyes and hear it in the tunes with which he answered her. Time passed, and in the Land of the Bells Carabella became truly contented, except for one thing—her loneliness for her father. Finally one day the girl felt she could suffer these feelings no longer. And she wept bitterly beside her beloved bells. Then the fairy appeared to her again, asking, "What troubles you so?"

"You have been so kind to me," said Carabella. "But today I am strung between harmony and discord, for I miss my father so. If he could share the language of the bells, I could play to him across the forest to let him know that I am safe and well—and about to be wed to the fair young man who met me halfway through the wood."

"That is not too much to ask," the fairy answered, and she disappeared.

That evening,
as the shepherd
drove his flock from
the hillside, he heard
a faint ringing more distant and
musical than the random tinkling
of the sheep's bells, and he stood still
and listened. To his amazement he could
understand the music's meaning, for it was
Carabella, ringing to him across the forest.
Instantly his heart lightened. The father's rejoicing
was doubled upon hearing that his dear child's wedding
should take place in his own land, for the fairy had decreed
it so. He hurried the sheep home so that he could take
Carabella's bells from their shelf and return to the hillside to
answer her.

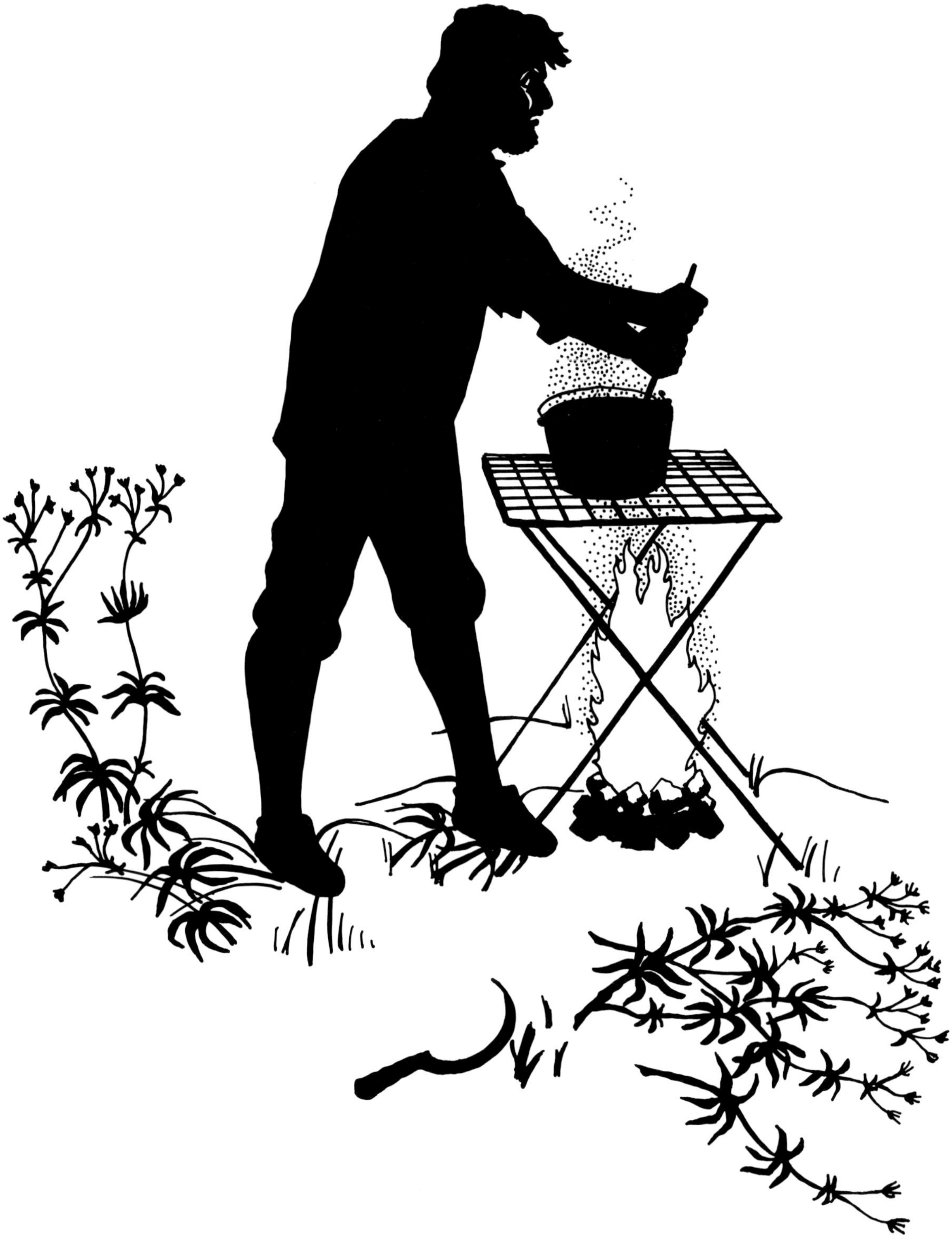

Chopping madder root in his garden, the spiteful weaver noticed as the shepherd passed by that his face had lost the worn look it had carried since his daughter's departure. "My daughter is well, and to be wed—here in our own land!" the shepherd called out joyfully. "I have heard from Carabella and I must reply."

Suddenly the fire of vengeance that still smoldered in the weaver's heart was by jealousy ignited anew. He stirred the wool in his simmering dyebath, and stalked the shepherd with his eyes. As Carabella's father made his way to the hillside with his daughter's bells, the weaver vowed that, since he himself had failed to win her, no man would ever wed Carabella.

Throngs of eager neighbors over every hill and vale made ready for the return of their beloved girl of the bells; and the shepherd taught them the musical language. On the day of the wedding, the forest was alive with the melodies of the arriving guests, and the hillside rang with rounds of welcoming greetings. But the weaver only clapped his hands over his ears and cursed the bride and groom.

Still hoping to spin the perfect plot to spoil everyone's rapture, he joined his neighbors waiting on the forest's edge to welcome the pair. It was then that he spotted, in Carabella's hands, a bouquet of tiny, white, bell-shaped flowers. A cruel smile spread across the weaver's lips as he culled from his knowledge of plants and dyes an oft forgotten fact . . . that the lily of the valley, so beautiful to the eye, is poison on the tongue! Whereupon he said to Carabella in his fondest tone, "I too will pick a sprig of lily by which to remember this happy day."

As the wedding couple led their guests to the hillside on which the ceremony was to take place, the weaver searched the forest's edge for a dainty lily—and plucked it from the ground, root and all. Unnoticed in the hillside throng, the weaver dropped the sprig of lily upon a rock, and crushed the root hard under his foot to release the most deadly poison. Then secretly soaking the damaged lily in the goblet that had been prepared for the ceremony, he smiled as the bitter juices mingled with the wine.

As the sun set, the ceremony began. In the hush, the only sounds that could be heard were the bride and groom ringing their vows, and the soft jingling of the sheep's bells on the next hillside. Looking into Carabella's eyes, the groom took a sip of wine from the goblet. But just as he was about to pass it to his bride, the silence was broken by the weaver's stunning laughter. Unable to contain his satisfaction, he cried out, "No man shall ever wed the shepherd's daughter!" The helpless onlookers gasped in unison as the groom collapsed to the ground, with his bride still clasping his lifeless hand.

With several of the wedding guests in passionate pursuit of him, the weaver ran to the forest cackling his cruel contentment. Then suddenly before him, glowing in a bed of pine needles, arose—a sprig of lily! Unable to bear the beauty of the little bells, he crushed them under his foot. Two more lilies arose ahead of the first, and he took two steps forward crushing them both. Now four arose. Each time he trampled the flowers their numbers doubled ahead of him.

Glistening in the moonlight, the path of tiny bells compelled his frantic feet onward and onward through the forest. Suddenly behind him the pursuing throng stopped short, for they saw where the path was leading him. Trying to crush the next lily before it arose, the weaver took his last step over a cliff and fell down, down to his death!

On the hillside the mournful tolling of the bells rang out the wordless grief of the bridegroom's loved ones. Tenderly Carabella cradled her lover's lifeless head in her lap. "Oh, why has the fairy abandoned you?" the shepherd wept beside her, burying his face in his hands. But Carabella shook the tears from her eyes and answered in a voice both tremulous and true, "She hasn't, Father."

Suddenly an extraordinary light arose from the ground, and the fairy appeared in the darkness. Without a word she plucked a sprig of lily from the bridal bouquet and kissed it lightly, turning the little white bells to silver. Then returning the sprig of bells to Carabella, the fairy dissolved in the darkness as quickly as her light had shone forth.

"Wait. . . . Please!" the shepherd called after the fairy, and his grieving neighbors echoed his despair.

But Carabella put a finger to her lips to hush the throng. Closing her eyes she lost herself to the deepening stillness until it had filled her depths. Then taking the pointed tip of one of the lily's broad green leaves, she ran it along the silver bells. The clarity of the little notes was so startling against the silent night that it awakened her lover out of death's sleep! How the bride and groom embraced one another and Carabella's dear father! And in the rejoicing that followed, the hills rang with music until dawn.

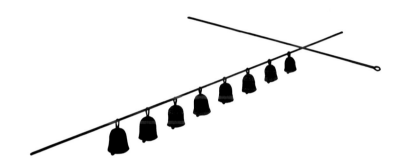

A NOTE TO PARENTS, GRANDPARENTS AND TEACHERS

The response of readers to the first edition of THE GATE OF DREAMS has been heartwarming, and I am delighted that a soft cover edition is now available.

I intended these original fairy stories for the broadest range of readers, and have been gratified to learn how popular the book has been as a family read-aloud. The stories have not been simplified for children, since I think it is in discovering words in context that our vocabularies broaden. However, since the silhouette characters perform the stories almost as if on stage, even the youngest family members can follow the action of these stories while listening to them.

Of course, the GATE OF DREAMS is also meant for the private enjoyment of readers of any age. Boys enjoy the stories as much as girls; and I have been pleased to hear from many men who, having once picked up the book, have found themselves moved to read from cover to cover.

THE GATE OF DREAMS has inspired creative writing projects in schools, in which teachers have used the book as a focal point for the study of fairy tales, culminating in the students writing and illustrating their own original stories. Since the term "fairy tale" is so often used as a catch-all for fantasy or for any tale involving magic, the following list of common characteristics of traditional fairy tales might prove useful to teachers interested in pursuing such a creative writing project with their students. It is my hope that the list might be of interest to others who simply find themselves intrigued by the fairy tale genre.

- *Fairy tales happen in a different place and time.* When we hear a beginning like "Far away and long ago there lived..." we are not only transported but given permission to suspend our disbelief. After all, in a different place and time, things might happen which could never happen in "our world".

- *The main characters are clearly "good" or "evil"*, allowing the child freedom from ambivalence while reading or listening to the story. Full-strength responses undiluted by doubt and deliberation are invited and even exacted from the reader when confronted with characters as cruel as the Queen in "Snow White", or as tender in spirit as Snow White herself.

- *The hero or heroine is faced with a difficult problem which may seem impossible to live with and impossible to solve.* The challenge may

87

require outwitting or outrunning a formidable foe like the Giant in "Jack and the Beanstalk"; or the challenge may require emotional endurance and faith, like that which Cinderella displayed in the face of injustice and degradation. But regardless of the particular trial facing the protagonist, hardship and suffering are as essential a part of fairy tales as they are unavoidable in our lives.

- *The stories are full of symbolic objects and events which have deep psychological meanings.* The thorns which grow up around the slumbering castle which encloses Briar Rose and all her world reinforce the feeling of adolescent withdrawal and defensiveness— a stage in life which, though it seems to last a hundred years, we must all endure at least once—and perhaps several times through our children. But whether we pick up on universal meanings or supply personal interpretations of our own, fairy stories are rich in symbolic raw material—very much, I think, like the fabric of dream imagery. (It is absolutely essential to keep in mind that there is no "correct" interpretation of a fairy tale, for its meanings are as varied and individual as each reader's innermost thoughts and emotions.)

- *As a fairy tale nears its conclusion, justice is done—fairy tale justice, that is*—wherein good qualities such as gentleness, bravery, loyalty, and cleverness are rewarded, and evildoers are punished in the most appropriate and satisfying ways. What could be more perfect than the witch in "Hansel and Gretel" burning to cinders in the very oven in which she planned to cook the lost children!?

- *A fairy tale ends in fulfillment for the protagonist.* In fact, sometimes the only thing setting a fairy tale apart from a myth, a fable, or a cautionary tale is the existence of a happy ending. Even the fairy tale's ending, however, is symbolic rather than literal. The "happily ever after" signifies hope to the child.

My convictions about the benefits of fairy tales in childhood and throughout our lives prompted the creation of THE GATE OF DREAMS. I believe that the magic of fairy tales, ironically enough, lies not so much in their fantasy but in their emotional reality. It is because they provide a looking glass reflection of our inner lives that they are so useful to us in childhood and beyond.

A NOTE TO PARENTS, GRANDPARENTS AND TEACHERS

By presenting the hero or heroine with a challenge which seems insurmountable, fairy tales acknowledge that life is not easy. These stories convey a difficult truth: that sometimes we will suffer long and hard before we find our way out of the woods. But at the same time, they reassure us that if we learn to trust ourselves, we will discover that somewhere within the rich range of our emotions, each of us "has what it takes" to create his own satisfying conclusions.

The fairy tale promise is simply and only this...that life will at last become richly rewarding to us because of what we ourselves become during the struggle.

Lillian Somersaulter Moats
1995

89

ACKNOWLEDGMENTS

The Cranbrook Educational Community is comprised of Cranbrook Academy of Art, Cranbrook Institute of Science and the Cranbrook Schools. I was inspired by the loveliness of Saarinen's architecture and the grace of Carl Milles' outdoor sculpture while attending Kingswood School Cranbrook and studying at the Young People's Art Center of the Cranbrook Academy of Art. The nearly inexpressible beauty which so long surrounded me has shaped my artistic sensibilities in more ways than I can describe. Still, in my heart of hearts it was the earlier and less tangible inspiration of Cranbrook Schools Brookside, instilled in my childhood through the simple gifts of nurturance, trust and love, that has provided me with a creative well-spring to which I endlessly return.

I wish to thank my mentors, Helen Southgate Williams and Glen Michaels, who have inspired me during and since my Cranbrook years. My gratitude extends to all those members of the Cranbrook Community and beyond who were actively involved in the realization of THE GATE OF DREAMS, most notably Margot Snyder, the book's producer. These individuals, along with my own family and the children of Brookside, have made real to me the words of Cranbrook's founder:

"The only way to have is to give,
The only way to keep is to share,
And the only thing worth finding
is opportunity"